2020 © Jay Cameron
Maximum Impact Publishing
Washington, D.C.

This book belongs to

_____

"Guess what!" Dad said to the twins. "We are going to Africa!"

"Why?" Darren questioned.

"Well, because I want you to know there are other places besides America."

"But Daddy, what is shown on television are those who don't have food or a place to live. It looks sad there," Destiny moaned.

"Oh no honey," Mom interuppted. "Some places are deprived in Africa, but not everywhere. It's a huge continent with many countries," Mom added as she walked to give Destiny a pat on her back. Darren and Destiny became excited about visiting new places. They were going to Ghana, a country that is almost twice the size of New York State.

To see actual footage of some of the places highlighted in the book, visit Jaycameron.com/traveladventures

The twins were excited, but the trip was a few weeks away. Every day, Darren and Destiny looked at the map and wondered what Africa was going to be like. Were they going to see lions, elephants, and giraffes? How would the food look and taste? Where were they going to sleep?

The night before the trip, Darren and Destiny could hardly sleep. The big day finally came, but before they could go to Africa, they had to go to the airport to get on an airplane.

As they waited in line at the airport, their mom handed to them their passports.

" These are special passes so that you can fly to another country, " Mom eagerly explained.

Darren and Destiny found lots of cool things to do on the plane. They watched movies, read books, and played games. When they looked out of the window, they saw how close the plane was to the clouds.

When they saw the ocean, Darren shouted, "Look at all the water!"

After flying all night, they landed in Accra, the capital of Ghana. While on their way to the hotel, they were amazed by the people who were selling goods next to the road. They sold things like foods, clothes, toys, and even furniture! Darren and Destiny had not seen anything like it. Destiny pointed to a little girl who was selling beautiful pottery.

To see actual footage of some of the places highlighted in the book, visit jaycameron.com/traveladventures

When they arrived at the hotel, they peered out of the window and saw people at the swimming pool.

Surprised, Darren yelled, "Look! It's a swimming pool and people are swimming in it!"

Mom laughed and said, "Yes, there are lots of beautiful swimming pools in Ghana."

Confused, Darren asked, "Why don't they show this part of Africa on television? I only saw sad things."

Mom nodded and answered, "I know honey, but I promise, you will see and learn a lot of new things on this trip!"

15

The next day, their tour guide, Nana, took them to the Dr. Kwame Nkrumah Museum. He was the first President of Ghana after it gained independence from British rule in 1957. Darren and Destiny saw his car and many items he used during his lifetime. They also learned about his favourite saying: "Forward ever, Backwards never".

"What is British rule?" Destiny asked.

"This is an excellent question, Destiny!" Dad answered. "We are going to learn more about it as we tour through Ghana."

Next, they visited Independence Square. A large monument was built to celebrate Ghana 's independence. It is easy to recognize because of the large black stars at the top. It is also the location where many official parades are held.

AD 1957

FREEDOM AND JUSTICE

The third place they visited was the W.E.B DuBois Centre. Dr. DuBois was born in 1868 and was an important person in America during the early 1900s. He was involved in the Civil Rights Movement and wrote many books. He moved to Ghana upon invitation from the president and to write. He died there in 1963. The family went to their hotel that night, thinking about everything they learned about Dr. DuBois.

The next day, Darren and Destiny went to The Art Centre in Accra. They met a man named Isaac who lived in Ghana.

"Are you ready to learn how to play African drums?" Isaac asked them.

Darren and Destiny both shouted, "Yeah!"

As Isaac showed them traditional ways to play the drum, Darren and Destiny excitedly laughed. They were having lots of fun!

"This is cool!" Destiny announced. "I wish all of my friends could do this."

"They can," Isaac assured as he cast the little girl a broad smile. "Take a drum home and teach them."

Next, they visited a place where artisans were making wood carvings and baskets.

"Look!" Darren shouted. "They are making the drums we just learned to play!"

"Yes," Destiny said. "And lots of other pretty things too!"
"Making and selling items is how they make money to survive," Mom said.

"They are really talented. It's amazing to watch. Most of them have been making these items since they were children like you!" Dad said.

To see actual footage of some of the places highlighted in the book, visit Jaycameron.com/traveladventures

The family visited a village near Kumasi where they learned about Adinkra Stamping. Adinkra symbols are used by the Ashanti tribe as a part of their tradition. Darren and Destiny helped to make the ink used for unique Adinkra stamps.

After they made stamps, they took part in an Ashanti naming ceremony at the Adanwomasi village.

"My ancestors were Ashanti," Dad said. "It would be really cool to get Ashanti names."

The twins became excited. Before they could get their names, they had to go through a ceremony, which involved members of the tribe washing their feet. Destiny giggled, as she was ticklish.

Members of the tribe performed a dance. It was wonderful. After the dance, Darren and Destiny learned that the names given were based on the day of the week they were born, which was on a Monday. Darren 's Ashanti name was Kojo because he 's a boy and Destiny 's name was Adwoa because she 's a girl.

Afterwards, they visited a local park. Darren and Destiny met Kofi, Emanuel, and Esi, who lived in Ghana. Destiny and Esi noticed that their hair texture looked a lot alike. When Esi learned that Destiny had just gotten an Ashanti name, her face lit up.

"I'm from the Fanti kingdom and my name shows that I was born on a Thursday!" she explained.

Darren, Kofi, and Emanuel talked about playing soccer and took a photo together.

Later, Darren and Destiny observed how Kente cloth was made using silk and cotton. They learned about the history of Kente cloth and the Ashanti meaning in the color patterns. That night, they went to bed excited about everything they had seen.

The next morning, Mom and Dad took the twins to Kakum National Park. Seven bridges that are more than 130 feet above the ground were in the park. The twins learned that the bridges were called a canopy walk because they connected the tree tops which gave access to the forest.

Ghana is one of the largest producers of cocoa in the world. When the family visited a local village, Phillip taught them about the many uses of the cocoa pod. He told them that not only does chocolate come from cocoa, but also black soap and cocoa butter. Darren and Destiny tasted the seeds.

"Don't swallow them," Mom said.

The seeds were sweet and tart. They didn't taste anything like chocolate.

LAST BATH

39

"Our next stop is going to be a bit sad," Mom explained after they finished learning about cocoa.

"Sad like we see on television at home?" Destiny asked.

"No sweetie. We're going to learn about slavery today." Darren and Destiny learned about slavery in school.

"We know all about that," Darren expressed.

Nana nodded and said, "Yes, but this is going to be different than what you read about in books."

He took them to the Slave River. They were told about those who were taken captive in Africa and brought to the river to be bathed and sold before they were led to one of the dungeons at the coast.

" What is a dungeon? " Destiny asked.

" We are headed there next, " Mom shared.

A few minutes later, they were standing in front of the Elmina slave dungeon. The dungeon was built by the Portuguese and is one of the few dungeons that still exists.

" This is a huge place, " Darren blurted.

" Yes son, with a very sad history, " Dad replied.

Nana explained that many of the enslaved captives were brought to the dungeon before they were placed on ships to be taken against their will to South, Central, and North America. He also explained how hard the living conditions were when someone was brought to the dungeon. Darren and Destiny had no idea how hard it was for people during slavery.

The family was shocked to see how terrible things were inside the dungeon. Mom began to cry as she imagined what the people had gone through before they passed the Door of No Return.

"Why did people put those who they captured in Africa into slavery?" asked Darren.

"Greed," Dad explained. "People do terrible, terrible things when they are greedy."

44

The next morning, the family visited Cape Coast. Darren and Destiny ate fresh coconuts and played in the water.

" This is one of the most beautiful beaches I ' ve ever seen honey, " Mom gushed to Dad.

" In some ways, Africa is like America, but in other ways it is vastly different, " he replied.

Later that evening, the family went to a lovely restaurant. Mom and Dad thought it was important to talk about slavery, the dungeons, and everything they saw. The twins had lots of questions. It was a moment when the family felt closer to each other.

As they ate and talked, Darren probed, "Mommy what kind of rice is this? It 's goooood!"

"It 's called Jollof Rice," Dad resolved.

"We love it!" the twins shouted.

It was finally time for them to return home. Destiny and Darren were sad because they did not want to leave. They had so much fun and learned a lot in Ghana. They could not wait to tell their friends about the beauty of Africa.

To see actual footage of some of the places highlighted in the book, visit jaycameron.com/traveladventures

50

Made in the USA
Columbia, SC
30 September 2020